Let's Play
TAG!

- 📖 Read the Page
- ▶ Read the Story

- ⭐ Game

- 🔁 Repeat

- ⬛ Stop

💻

Disney · PIXAR
BRAVE

I am Merida, princess of Dunbroch, and this is my story.

My father, King Fergus is a brilliant warrior who long ago fought the monstrous bear, Mor'du, and lost his leg. It was legendary!

My mum, Queen Elinor, is the picture of diplomacy and etiquette. She has always prepared me to follow in her footsteps, practically planning my whole life. But all I wanted was to be free of duties and have adventures!

One day it became truly bad—the day she announced
that a competition would be held for my hand in marriage!

"You can't make me!"
I shouted.

It was too late, though. The lords of the three clans had brought their sons to compete for my hand—numpties, the lot of them. But I wasn't ready, and Mum, she wouldn't listen. So I decided to enter the competition to shoot for my own hand.

I won, too! But Mum was furious.

She dragged me into the castle, saying it would be fire and sword if I didn't set things right. I tried to explain that it was *my* life.

"I'll never be like you!" I cried.

With my sword, I slashed our family tapestry, putting a rip right between Mum and me.

I ran straight away, riding Angus deep into the forest. There I came upon a wood-carving woman, but I could tell she was really a witch.

I told the Witch, "If I could just change my mum, then my life would be better."

I even agreed to buy all her carvings in exchange for one spell. The Witch finally agreed, and she told me of a prince who had asked for the strength of ten men. He was forever changed after visiting her. Then, she made me a spell cake.

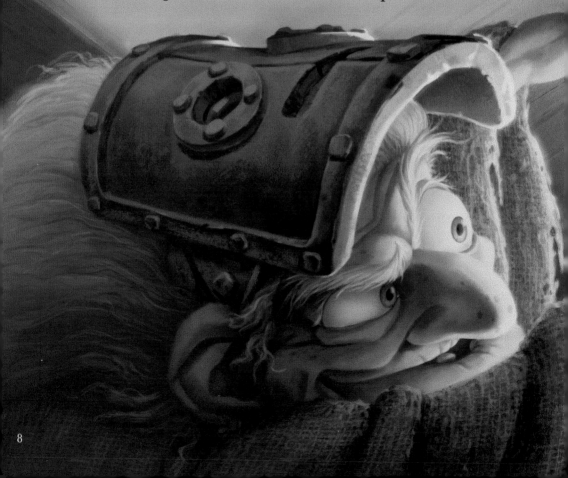

 I rushed home and gave Mum the cake.

"It's a peace offering. I made it for you!"

She took a bite. I watched, waiting for her to change her mind. But instead of calling off the marriage, she became very ill … and turned into a bear! I didn't ask for *that!* We had to find that scaffy witch.

After searching for her in the forest, we found her cottage. The Witch was gone, but she left a clue in her cauldron:

"Fate be changed, look inside, mend the bond, torn by pride."

I simply didn't understand.

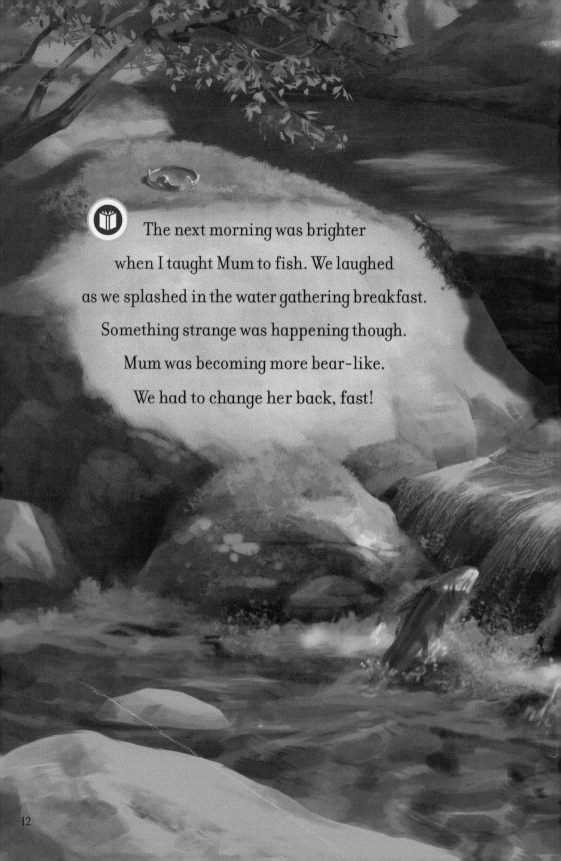

The next morning was brighter
when I taught Mum to fish. We laughed
as we splashed in the water gathering breakfast.
Something strange was happening though.
Mum was becoming more bear-like.
We had to change her back, fast!

13

While looking for the Witch, we discovered some ancient castle ruins. Inside was a stone tablet picturing four princes, with one split off from the rest: a prince who had fought his brothers!

Suddenly, out of the darkness, Mor'du attacked! The ruins were his home! The Witch's prince had become the monstrous bear Mor'du! Mum saved me, and we raced away from him.

I told Mum I understood now—"Mend the bond torn by pride." I had to mend the family tapestry. But first we had to go back to the castle to get it.

Inside, the clan leaders were fighting over which son I should marry. They were practically at war—because of *my* actions! How could I sneak Mum past them all? So I tried to say what Mum would say, while she hid in the back of the room.

Just as I was about to agree to choose my future husband, Mum signaled me to stop. She wanted me to find love in my own time. As it turned out, the lads wanted the same thing! Everyone was happy.

But it didn't last. As Mum and I tried to repair the tapestry,
Dad found us. He thought Mum was a wild bear.

He wouldn't listen to reason. Dad gathered the clans
and chased Mum into the forest.

I followed on Angus while repairing the torn tapestry. When I found Dad and all the men, they had cornered Mum.

"I won't let you hurt my mum!" I yelled.

Suddenly, Mor'du appeared and attacked. When he started after me, Mum broke free and charged him. After a wild battle, Mum conquered the beast for good.

I wrapped Mum in the tapestry, but the spell was unbroken. I didn't know what else to do.

I told her "I just want you back. I want you back, Mummy, I-I love you."

As I wept into Mum's fur, the light broke, and I felt Mum's hand brush through my hair.

"Mum, you're back! You've changed!" I cried.

"No, sweetheart, we did," she replied.

It was true. We both had changed, and learned to accept each other just exactly as we were.

❧ Word List ❧

bill	sip	deep
still	drip	sleep
chill	whip	sheep

ill

s
d
b

23

The Road to Understanding

Merida *or* Elinor